Piper the Elf Trains Santa

by
Colleen Driscoll

illustrated by
Brian Dumm

Jensen,
May All Your Christmases Be Magical!
Colleen Driscoll
2012

Headline Kids
an imprint of Headline Books, Inc.
Terra Alta, WV

Piper the Elf Trains Santa

by Colleen Driscoll
illustrated by Brian Dumm

copyright ©2013 Colleen Driscoll

To order additional copies of this book, or
for book publishing information, or to contact the author:

Headline Kids
P. O. Box 52
Terra Alta, WV 26764

Tel: 800-570-5951
Email: mybook@headlinebooks.com
www.headlinebooks.com
www.headlinekids.com

Published by Headline Books
Headline Kids is an imprint of Headline Books

ISBN-13: 978-0-938467-56-4

Library of Congress Control Number: 2012947095

Driscoll, Colleen.
  Piper the elf trains santa / by Colleen Driscoll ; illustrations By Brian Dumm.
    p. cm.
  ISBN 978-0-938467-56-4
  1. Exercise--Fiction 2. Health--Fiction. 3.Christmas stories. 4. Friendship.
  I. Dumm, Brian, ill. II. Title.

PRINTED IN THE UNITED STATES OF AMERICA

*Dedicated to
my husband, Paul,
and my children,
Kevin, Ashley,
Brian and Brooke*

Piper the Elf lived at the North Pole
with her mother and father, and of course,
Santa Claus.

Piper loved to go outside in the snow and play
with the other elves. Some days they would go
sledding. Other days they would build snowmen,
and sometimes the elves would throw snowballs
at each other.

One day while Piper was helping her father make toys in Santa's workshop, Mrs. Claus came up to the little elf.

"Piper," she said, "I really need your help."

Piper replied, "What do you need, Mrs. Claus?"

"Santa does not fit into his suit anymore and Christmas is in one month," she said. "He is eating too many cookies. The buttons are popping off his clothes. Would you exercise with Santa?" Mrs. Claus asked, "I want you to be his personal trainer."

"Sure," said Piper. She didn't know what a personal trainer did, but she wanted to help Santa. "Thank you," said Mrs. Claus. "I will tell him to come to your house tomorrow afternoon. Good-bye."

"You are welcome, Mrs. Claus. Good-bye," said Piper.

9

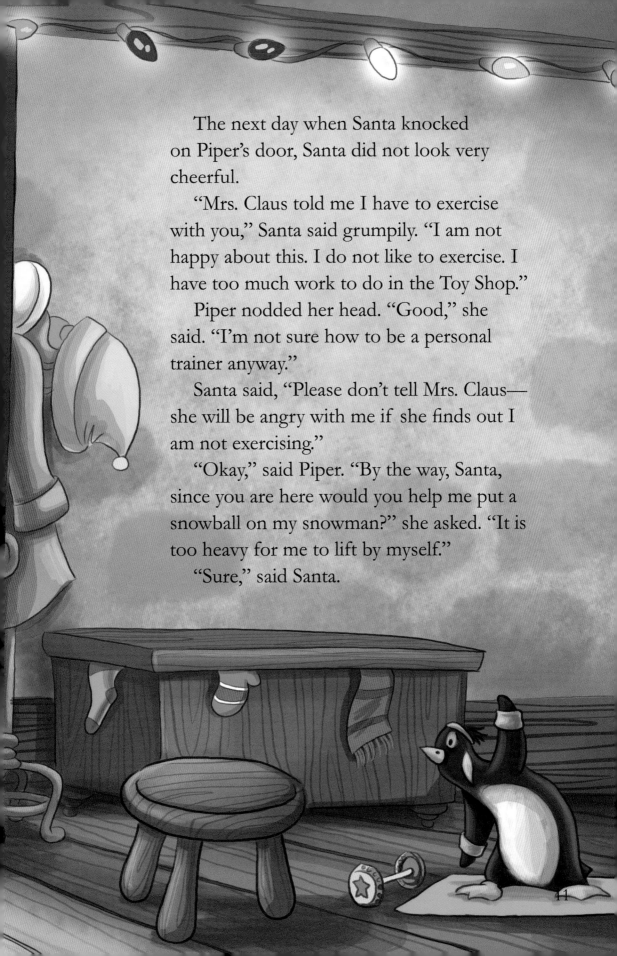

The next day when Santa knocked on Piper's door, Santa did not look very cheerful.

"Mrs. Claus told me I have to exercise with you," Santa said grumpily. "I am not happy about this. I do not like to exercise. I have too much work to do in the Toy Shop."

Piper nodded her head. "Good," she said. "I'm not sure how to be a personal trainer anyway."

Santa said, "Please don't tell Mrs. Claus—she will be angry with me if she finds out I am not exercising."

"Okay," said Piper. "By the way, Santa, since you are here would you help me put a snowball on my snowman?" she asked. "It is too heavy for me to lift by myself."

"Sure," said Santa.

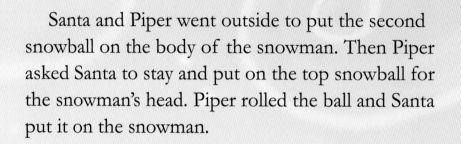

Santa and Piper went outside to put the second snowball on the body of the snowman. Then Piper asked Santa to stay and put on the top snowball for the snowman's head. Piper rolled the ball and Santa put it on the snowman.

"Your snowman looks lonely," said Santa. "Let's make another one." Santa helped Piper roll the balls and together they built another snowman. Piper said it was *Mrs. Snowman*. "Now you need a whole family of snowmen," said Santa.

One of Piper's friends, Skinner, was walking by Piper's house and saw the snowmen. Skinner asked if he could help.

So Piper, Santa and Skinner spent the afternoon building snowmen. When it was time for Santa to go back to work, he told Piper that he had a lot of fun.

"Come tomorrow," Piper told him, "and we will go sledding."

"I haven't gone sledding in years," Santa told the two elves. "I hope I remember what to do."

The next afternoon, Santa came to
Piper's house and went sled riding with
Piper and three more elves—Ricky,
Niki, and Miles. Santa was surprised he
remembered how to sled. He had so much
fun going down the hill and walking back
up the hill while talking and laughing with
the little elves. They sledded all day.

Each afternoon Santa came over to play with Piper since Mrs. Claus thought they were exercising together anyway. Some days they built snow forts. Several times they made snowballs and ran around the snow forts chasing each other with them. Other days they made snow angels in the snow. They even tried skiing and snow tubing down the hills around the Toy Shop. Santa enjoyed playing with Piper and the other little elves.

One afternoon a week before Christmas, Santa came to Piper's house. Santa looked worried. "Mrs. Claus thinks I have been exercising with you, Piper. She doesn't know that we were just having fun playing in the snow. When Mrs. Claus gets out my red suit for me to try on tomorrow she will know that I have not been exercising. What will I say?"

Piper thought and thought and then laughed to herself. "Do not worry, Santa," she said. "Let's go have some more fun today and we will think of something later."

So Santa, Piper and the little elves played all
afternoon running in the snow, chasing each
other and having a giant snowball fight. Santa
was so tired when he left that he forgot about
trying on his red suit.

The next day, Mrs. Claus took Santa's red suit out of his closet and asked Santa to try it on to see if the suit fit him. To Santa's surprise the suit was a little loose!

"How did this happen?" Santa wondered aloud in amazement.

"Because you have been exercising at Piper's house this past month," said Mrs. Claus. "That is how it happened."

When Santa went to see Piper that afternoon he told Piper about his red suit fitting him. "It was even a little loose," Santa laughed. "I don't understand. We didn't exercise. We just played every day and had lots of fun."

Piper laughed and said, "Santa, you WERE exercising. You exercised when you played."

Santa looked at Piper in amazement. Santa had a twinkle in his eyes. Then he started his jolly, HO, HO, HO laugh. "You are such a tricky personal trainer, Piper," Santa said. "I had so much fun playing with you that I didn't even know I was exercising."

29

Piper looked at Santa and giggled, "Everyone can exercise and still have fun."

North Pole Exercises

Santa Jacks

Penguin Pass

Snowflake Stretch

Santa Sprint

Ho Ho Hula

Jingle Jump

Fun and Healthy Recipes for the Holidays

Candy Cane Cocoa

Put 2 teaspoons sugar in a cup
Add 1 teaspoon unsweetened cocoa
Add 3 teaspoons water
Heat in microwave for 15 seconds
Add 1% milk to fill cup
Stir and heat in microwave
  for 1 min.
Top with whipped crème, chocolate
  sprinkles
Add a candy cane as a stirrer. Enjoy!

Reindeer Crunch Treats

In a re-sealable plastic bag, mix:
½ cup raisins
½ cup pretzels (sticks or twists)
¼ cup peanuts
¼ cup sliced almonds
2 teaspoons sunflower seeds
1 cup unsweetened oat
or wheat cereal
Close bag, shake, carry
with you to eat

Colleen Driscoll grew up in western Pennsylvania where she earned her B.S. degree at Indiana University of Pennsylvania. After starting a family, she taught music in Stafford, Virginia. Though she always enjoyed reading stories to her children, Colleen did not begin to write down her own stories until her children were in school. She currently lives with her husband and four children in Bridgeport, WV. She enjoys spending time with her family, reading, singing, crafts and composing music. This is her first children's book.

Brian Caleb Dumm is an artist-illustrator, writer, and educator from west/central Pennsylvania. Practicing professionally since 2005, his work has been published nationally and internationally. Brian is a graduate of The Pennsylvania State University, and also has certification/degrees from The Columbus College of Art and Design, Indiana University of Pennsylvania, and Saint Francis University. For more information please visit www.bcdummillustration.com.

Author photo by Mark Kiger